Star Blanket

Star Blanket

by Pat Brisson

Illustrated by Erica Magnus

Sweet dreams!
Pat Brisson
♡

BOYDS MILLS PRESS

Boyds Mills Press, Inc.
A Highlights Company
815 Church Street
Honesdale, Pennsylvania 18431
Printed in China

Publisher Cataloging-in-Publication Data (U.S.)

Brisson, Pat.
Star blanket / by Pat Brisson ; illustrated by Erica Magnus. — 1st ed.
[32] p. : col. ill. ; cm.
Summary: A story about a father's bedtime story.
ISBN 1-56397-889-X
1.Bedtime — Fiction — Juvenile literature. 2. Fathers – Fiction — Juvenile literature.
(1.Bedtime — Fiction. 2. Fathers – Fiction.) I. Magnus, Erica. II. Title.
[E] 21 PZ7.B78046Sta 2003
2002117203
First edition, 2003

Book design by Amy Drinker, Aster Designs
The text of this book is set in 16-point Stone Serif.
The illustrations are done in watercolors.

Visit our Web site at www.boydsmillspress.com

10 9 8 7 6 5 4 3 2 1

For all my Gerity relatives, here on earth and home in Heaven;

for my brother Tom McDonough and my niece Laura;

and for my son Gabriel and my daughter-in-law, Vanessa,

the newest star on our family's Star Blanket

—P. B.

For Karen and Kaya

—E. M.

When Laura goes to bed each night, she takes the Star Blanket with her—a special blanket that is deep dark blue with forty-one white stars and a smooth satin border on all four sides. It's an old blanket, with holes and almost-holes so Laura can see the moonlight right through parts of it.

On the nights Dad puts her to bed, he makes a deal with her. If she can brush her teeth, put on her pajamas, and get into bed before he counts to fifty, there will be time for a story. Laura always asks for the story of the Star Blanket.

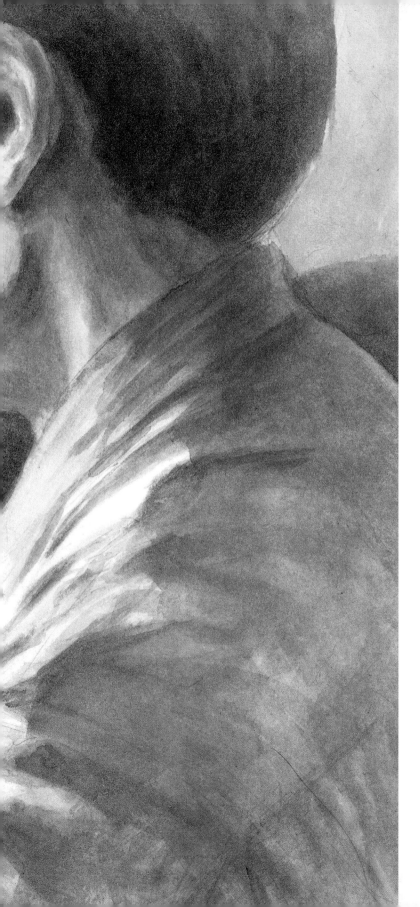

She snuggles under her covers and waits for her father's deep, soft voice to begin, as he always does. "When I was four years old, your Aunt Patty was born."

"Only you didn't call her Aunt Patty, did you, Daddy?" Laura asks, although she knows the answer.

"No, you're right. We called her Pat, and sometimes my father called her The Caboose."

"Because she was the last one, right?"

"Right. Now, when Pat was a few weeks old, it was time for her to be baptized. We all piled into the old green DeSoto and drove down to Saint James Church. It was a big old church that creaked when the wind blew, and when the sun shone through the stained-glass windows, spots of color appeared on the pews and along the aisles.

"Monsignor McCorristan was the priest. He said the prayers and blessed her, and when he poured the holy water on Pat's head, she never even cried.

"On the way back to the house, Aunt Anna and Aunt Betty and Gram all said what a wonderful baby Pat was. Then they told how on my christening day, I had hollered so long and loud that my face turned red and the priest almost had to shout so the prayers could be heard. Everybody laughed except for me.

"Then more relatives came, and there was eating and talking and everyone said how good Baby Pat was to sleep right through it. The men smoked cigars on the porch, and my aunts borrowed aprons from my mother and helped in the kitchen.

"When it was time for my mother to open Pat's presents, she let me help take off the wrapping paper and ribbon. I thought maybe one would be for me, but they were all for Pat.

"Finally I asked, 'Don't I get any?' My aunts all laughed. But my grandmother held out a package without a card.

"'This one is for you, Tommy,' she said. It was wrapped in tissue paper, and I opened it quickly.

"Inside was the Star Blanket—deep dark blue with forty-one white stars and a smooth satin border on all four sides. The material in the stars exactly matched the material in the scarf my grandmother wore around her neck.

"It was a nice blanket, but what I really wanted was a pair of cowboy boots like Hopalong Cassidy's. I must have looked disappointed because just then my Uncle Jim asked me if I wanted to walk to Ceasar's for an ice-cream cone with sprinkles. I liked Ceasar's because it had a soda fountain with green leather stools that you could spin around on while you waited for your cones.

"When we got back to the house, I thanked my grandmother for the blanket just like my Uncle Jim had told me I should. Then my gram said there was something I should know about the blanket.

"'What's that?' I asked her, and she said, 'Every star on the blanket has its own name, and if you can say good night to all of them, you'll never have trouble falling asleep.' Then she said, 'Would you like to know what their names are?'

"Of course I said yes.

"When she started to name them, I realized they were named after my grandparents, aunts, uncles, and cousins. The very last two names were mine and Pat's.

"I couldn't remember all of them at first because I was so little. But every time Gram came over, we'd practice, and pretty soon I could name them all. At Christmas, when all my relatives came to visit, Gram said, 'Name the stars on the Star Blanket, Tommy.'

"When I finished, everyone clapped, and my Uncle Dave gave me a silver dollar and said, 'And see that you don't forget a single one.'"

"And you never did forget, did you, Daddy?" Laura asks.

"No, I never did," he tells her.

"And it still helps you fall asleep?"

"Sure," he says. "Just listen."

And starting at the left-hand corner, he begins naming them in a slow, quiet voice. "Good night, Gram and Grandpop. Good night, Aunt Betty and Uncle Joe. Good night, Uncle Bill and Aunt Florrie. Good night, Uncle Low and Aunt Tess. Good night, Aunt Marie and Uncle Leo. Good night, Uncle Eddy and Aunt Ruth. Good night, Uncle Dave and Aunt Marie. Good night, Mom and Dad. Good night, Aunt Anna and Uncle Dinny. Good night, Uncle Leon and Aunt Marie. Good night, Uncle Jim."

He shuts off the lamp next to Laura's bed. Patches of moonlight fall on the blanket and floor.

"Now the cousins," says Laura.

"Yes, the cousins," he says. "Good night, Frannie, Mary Jane, Joey, Betty Ann, and Jimmy. Good night, Billy, Joan, and Sis. Good night, Bobby. Good night, Janie and Eileen. Good night, Mary Ann, Susan, Monica, and Leon. Good night, Mary Beth, Kathy, Kevin, Tom, and Pat."

"The Caboose," Laura says sleepily.

"The Caboose," her father
repeats in a whisper. "Just
like you."

He leans over to kiss her
cheek. "Good night, Laura,"
he says.